RABBIT RACE

Books in the Animal Ark Pets series

1 Puppy Puzzle
2 Kitten Crowd
3 Rabbit Race
4 Hamster Hotel

BEN M. BAGLIO

RABBIT RACE

Illustrated by
Paul Howard

Cover Illustration by
Chris Chapman

A
LITTLE APPLE
PAPERBACK

SCHOLASTIC INC.

New York Toronto London Auckland Sydney
Mexico City New Delhi Hong Kong

Special thanks to Helen Magee.
Thanks also to C.J. Hall, B.Vet.Med., M.R.C.V.S., for reviewing
the veterinary material contained in this book.

ISBN 0-439-05160-6

Text copyright © 1996 by Ben M. Baglio.
Illustrations copyright © 1996 by Paul Howard.

12 11 10 9 8 7 6   1 2 3 4/0

Printed in the U.S.A.   40

First Scholastic trade paperback printing, April 1999

Contents

1. New Arrivals 1
2. Jack 11
3. Animal Antics 22
4. A Surprise for James 33
5. Visiting 44
6. Getting Ready 57
7. The *Cheetah* 66
8. Hoppy's New Home 77
9. The Race 92
10. Runaway Rabbit! 107

1

New Arrivals

"Let's take Blackie to Lilac Cottage," Mandy Hope said to her friend James Hunter as they came out of school on Friday afternoon.

Blackie was James's black Labrador puppy. Mandy and James had house-trained him. Now they were trying obedience training. But that wasn't so easy.

"Good idea," said James. "I want to see if we can teach him to fetch. He's still a little afraid of Benji, so it's difficult to train him at home."

Benji was the Hunters' cat. He was still a little jealous of Blackie.

"Poor Benji," Mandy said as they walked down Main Street in Welford. "I think he feels left out."

James nodded. "I know," he said. "But it won't be for long — now that your grandma and grandpa are letting us use their backyard. It's very nice of them."

"Grandma and Grandpa love Blackie," Mandy said firmly. "They're happy to have him there. It's no problem."

Mandy never thought any animal was a problem — she loved them all. Both her parents were vets so she'd been brought up surrounded by all sorts of animals. James looked up at her and shoved his glasses further up his nose. He was a year younger than Mandy, but he was her best friend. Probably because he liked animals nearly as much as she did!

"Bye, Mandy! Bye, James!" Sarah Drummond called as she got into her mother's car outside the school gates. "Have a good weekend!"

"Tell Licorice we were asking about him!" Mandy called back.

Sarah and James had gotten puppies at the same time. Her puppy, Licorice, was one of Blackie's brothers.

Mandy and James waved as Sarah's mom drove off.

"Blackie and Benji will be fine together once they get used to each other," Mandy said to James.

"And once Blackie is more obedient," said James.

"We'll get Grandma to have a word with him," said Mandy. "She seems to be able to do anything with Blackie."

James grinned. "Look!" he said, pointing across the road.

Peter Foster, one of Mandy's classmates, was just opening his front gate. He staggered back as a hairy bundle of brown and gray fur hurled itself at him. It was Timmy, Peter's terrier.

"I wonder if your grandma could do anything with Timmy," James said.

Mandy giggled. "I doubt it," she said. "Timmy is something else."

They reached the general store. From here Mandy and James went different ways. Mandy lived in an old stone cottage called Animal Ark at one end of the village and James lived in a modern house at the other end.

The cottage was not just Mandy's home. Her parents' clinic was attached to it, which was where the name came from. Mandy always looked forward to going home after school to see how the animals were doing — and to check on any new arrivals.

"See you later," James said to Mandy.

Just then there was a rumbling sound and an enormous van came down Main Street and pulled up outside the store.

The driver leaned out and pushed his cap back on his head.

"Can you tell me if we're anywhere near Hobart's Corner?" he asked Mandy and James.

They looked up at him in surprise. There was another man in the truck with him. On the side of the van, in big red letters, were the words RAPID REMOVALS.

"Oh," said Mandy. "Is somebody moving into Hobart's?"

The man smiled. "Somebody is moving in — if I can find the place."

"Oh, sorry," Mandy said. "If you go down to the end of the road and turn left, you can't miss it. It's a big old house; the gate is right on the corner."

"It's falling apart," said James. "It's been empty for ages."

The driver looked at the other man. "Just as long as we can get the furniture in, that's all we care about," he said. "Thanks a lot for your help."

Before Mandy could ask him any more questions, he drove off.

A bell rang as the door of the store opened behind them.

"Now what was that all about?" asked Mrs. McFarlane.

Mr. and Mrs. McFarlane ran the general store. Mandy thought the store was the best shop in the village. It sold comics and candy and all kinds of things. Mandy and James had even gotten Blackie's first collar and leash there.

"Somebody is moving into Hobart's Corner," said Mandy.

Mrs. McFarlane looked surprised. "Really?" she said. "After all this time. And I never heard

a word about it! I wonder who bought that old place." She disappeared back into the shop to tell Mr. McFarlane.

James and Mandy looked at each another.

"Mrs. McFarlane hears about *everything* that goes on in the village," said Mandy. "How did she miss this news?"

James shrugged. "Beats me," he said. "Why don't we go and see? Hobart's Corner is on the way to Lilac Cottage. I can meet you there."

Mandy ran all the way home and rushed through the door of Animal Ark.

"You'll never guess," she said.

"Guess what?" said Jean Knox, the receptionist, looking up from a pile of forms.

Mandy leaned against the receptionist desk and tried to get her breath back.

"A moving truck stopped outside the general store to ask directions to Hobart's Corner," she said, her eyes shining. "Someone is going to live there at last."

Jean raised her eyebrows in surprise and her

glasses slid down her nose and off the end. They swung on the chain around her neck as Jean shook her head.

"Well, now," she said. "And I thought that old house would never be sold."

"I want to tell Mom and Dad," said Mandy, jumping up. "Are they very busy?"

"Your dad's got a patient with him," Jean replied. "And your mom has gone to a calving up at Baildon Farm. But she said she'd be back in time to make dinner."

"Oh, good!" said Mandy. "Dad tries his best, but he just isn't as good a cook as Mom."

"And just what's wrong with my cooking?" said a voice from the door of the clinic.

Mandy whirled around. Dr. Adam Hope was standing there, smiling his lopsided smile.

"Oops!" said Mandy.

Dr. Adam laughed. "Caught you there, Mandy," he said.

Mandy noticed her dad was holding something small and furry.

"It's Ginny!" she said. "Is she better?"

Ginny had been a very sick little guinea pig when she first came to Animal Ark. Her teeth were very overgrown and she couldn't eat properly.

"I've trimmed her teeth and she's eating like a horse now," said Dr. Adam.

"Oh, Ginny," Mandy said, stroking the guinea pig's reddish-brown coat. "Pam will be so pleased."

The little animal looked up at her with its big dark eyes. Pam Stanton was in Mandy's class at

school and she had been really worried about Ginny.

"Oh, Dad, I've got really exciting news," said Mandy.

She told her father all about the moving truck and Hobart's Corner.

"Do you think the new people at Hobart's will have pets?" she said.

Jean Knox laughed. "Most nine-year-olds would wonder if they had children," she said.

"But our Mandy is more interested in their pets," Dr. Adam said.

Mandy shook her fair hair out of her eyes. "Of course I want to know if they have any children."

Jean perched her glasses on her nose and looked over the top of them at Mandy.

"Could that be because the more children there are, the more pets there will be?" she asked.

Mandy smiled widely at both of them. "How did you guess?" she grinned.

2

Jack

"Do you see anybody?" asked Mandy as she and James peered through the tall iron gates at Hobart's Corner.

James shook his head and gave Blackie's leash a tug, trying to get him to heel. But Blackie had other ideas. He was busy sniffling the grass, searching out all sorts of interesting smells.

"I can see a car," James said. "But the moving truck is gone. Blackie, behave!"

"He can't help it," said Mandy, smiling down at the gangly black puppy. "He's growing up so fast and there's so much for him to learn. He's interested in everything."

"I guess so," said James, his eyes still on the house. "I always thought that house looked really spooky."

Mandy looked at the tall, dark building. The paint on the window frames was peeling and the garden was badly overgrown.

"That's just because it's been empty so long," she said. "Dad says the last person to live in it was an old army captain. He moved away five years ago to live with his daughter."

"I don't remember him," said James.

"We were only little," Mandy said. "His name was Captain Hobart. That's why this was called Hobart's Corner."

Blackie gave a muffled bark and began to scrabble at the bottom of the gate.

"What now?" asked James, picking him up.

But Mandy had seen what was attracting Blackie.

"Look," she said. "There is somebody in the backyard. It looks like a little boy."

"Where?" said James.

Mandy pointed. "Sitting in that apple tree," she said. "He's watching us."

Mandy raised her hand and waved. "Hi, there!" she called. "What's your name?"

The boy continued to look at them, but he didn't speak.

"Maybe he didn't hear you," said James.

Mandy shook her head. "He heard all right," she said. "He just didn't answer."

Just then a woman came around the side of the house. She was dressed in faded jeans and a baggy sweater and her hair was tied back with a scarf. Her face was streaked with dust.

"Oh, hi!" she said as she saw Mandy and James at the gate. "You haven't seen a little boy, have you?" She looked worried. "I told him not to go out of the yard. The gate wasn't open, was it?"

Mandy shook her head and pointed at the boy in the apple tree. "Is that him?" she said.

"Oh, there you are, Jack!" said the woman. "You scared me, disappearing like that." She smiled at Mandy and James then turned back to Jack. "Come down out of there. You've got visitors."

Jack scrambled down out of the tree and stood for a moment looking at Mandy and James. He looked about six or seven years old. Mandy drew in her breath when she saw his face. He had been crying.

"I don't want visitors," he said. "I hate this place. I didn't want to come here. Leave me alone!"

And with that, he raced off across the grass and disappeared around the side of the house.

Mandy and James looked at the woman, embarrassed.

She smiled at them and drew a hand across her forehead. It left a long, dusty streak.

"Oh, dear," she said. "I wonder if this move was a good idea after all. Jack isn't happy about it."

Mandy and James looked at each other. They didn't know what to say.

"He'll get used to it," Mandy said at last. "Once he makes friends. Welford's a really good place to live."

The woman smiled. "I hope so," she said. Then she looked thoughtful. "He's going to start at the village school on Monday," she said. "I hope he'll be all right."

James smiled. "We go there, too," he said. "Tell Jack he's come at a good time. We've got the school picnic soon. That's always a lot of fun."

"And we'll keep an eye on Jack at school if you like," said Mandy.

The woman looked really grateful. "Thank you. That would be terrific," she said. Then she looked around. "I must go and find him. Goodness knows where he's run off to now."

She turned away, then turned back. "I forgot to ask your names," she said.

Mandy and James told her and she smiled. "I'm Mrs. Gardiner," she said. "Jack is seven — he's usually the friendliest little boy. I just hope he gets over this." She looked at Blackie at James's side. "But I don't expect seeing your puppy helped. Oh, dear, we've got such a lot of work to do."

Mandy and James watched as she walked away over the grass.

"She seems nice," said James.

Mandy nodded. "But Jack is really unhappy," she said. "Did you notice he'd been crying?"

"And what did she mean about Blackie not helping?" said James.

Mandy shrugged. "We've got a lot to find out about the Gardiners," she said. "And I know the perfect place to start."

"Where?" said James.

"Grandma!" said Mandy. "If she doesn't know something about the Gardiners, then nobody will!"

* * *

17

Grandma and Grandpa were working on their vegetable garden when Mandy and James arrived.

"Now you keep out of my beans, young Blackie," Grandpa said, leaning down to give Blackie a pat.

Blackie looked up at him and gave a short bark.

"I don't know whether that's a yes or a no," Grandma said. She looked at Mandy and James. "You two look as if you're bursting with news."

Mandy picked up a hoe and began to weed between the lines of beans.

"It's the new people at Hobart's Corner," she said. "They've got a little boy, but he seems really unhappy."

Grandma nodded and leaned on her hoe.

"I went there this afternoon with some cookies," she said.

"Nobody ever moves in around here without a plate of your grandma's cookies to help them along," Grandpa said with a wink.

"You know how it is," said Grandma. "Unpacking makes people hungry."

"And what did you find out about the Gardiners?" Mandy asked.

Grandma shook her head. "They've decided to do a lot of work on that house," she said. "They're hoping to turn it into a country guest house."

"But Hobart's Corner is falling apart," said James.

Grandpa nodded. "It seems Mr. Gardiner is going to fix it up."

"Wow!" said Mandy. "That'll take forever."

"And that isn't their only problem," Grandma said. "Little Jack didn't want to move in the first place, especially just after his dog died."

"What?" said Mandy, looking up from her hoeing.

Grandma nodded. "It was really sad," she said. "He had a dog named Fred, but Fred got very sick and died just before they moved here."

"That's awful," said James, looking down at Blackie. He bent down and gave the dog a cuddle. "I know how I'd feel if anything happened to Blackie."

"That explains why Mrs. Gardiner said seeing Blackie would upset him," said Mandy. "Oh, poor Jack. No wonder he's so unhappy."

Grandma looked at her. "Maybe you could try to make friends with him," she said.

Mandy nodded. "Of course we will," she said.

"But we can't force him to be friends," said James. "He doesn't seem to want us around."

Mandy looked thoughtful. "What if Jack had another pet?" she said. "Nobody could be unhappy if they had a pet to look after."

Grandpa looked doubtful. "It might be difficult to replace Jack's dog," he said.

Mandy shook her head. "I wasn't thinking about replacing Fred," she said. "I was just thinking about Jack having a new kind of pet."

"Like what?" asked James.

Mandy frowned. "I don't know yet," she said. "I'll think about it. I'll have to find out what Jack is like."

"How will you do that if he won't even talk to you?" said James.

Mandy shrugged. "I'll think of a way," she said. "Once he has a pet to care for, a pet that will love him back, he'll be much happier. You'll see."

3

Animal Antics

Mandy craned her neck, trying to see down to the front of the school assembly hall.

"Who are you looking for?" whispered James.

Mandy turned to him. It was Monday morning. She had been thinking a lot about Jack over the weekend.

"I'm looking for Jack," she said. "Remember, we said we'd keep an eye on him."

"And we will — if he'll let us," said James.

The younger children were lined up at the front of the hall.

"There he is," said Mandy. "Look, he's talking to Laura Baker."

James smiled. "Maybe he's made a friend already," he said. "Laura is really nice. She's very excited now because one of her rabbits is having babies."

Mandy nodded. "Fluffy's babies are due any day," she said. "Maybe she's telling Jack about it."

But James shook his head. "Maybe she is, but Jack doesn't seem interested. Look. He's stopped talking now."

Mandy watched as the little boy's head drooped. "He looks really sad, James."

James nodded, "We'll make sure we see him at recess," he said. "And we'll try to cheer him up."

Just then Mrs. Garvie, the principal, called the room to attention.

"As you know we will be having the school picnic soon," she said. "And I want you all to think of a theme for the day. I'm looking for suggestions." Her eyes twinkled. "Though we've had so many over the years I don't know if you can come up with anything new."

The students of Welford Village School had a picnic on Beacon Hill every summer and every year there was a different theme. Last year it had been pirates and they'd had games like "walking the plank" and "tug-of-war."

Mandy stuck her hand in the air and waved it frantically.

Mrs. Garvie looked at her. "Have you got a suggestion, Mandy?" she said. "Already?"

Mandy nodded. "Oh, Mrs. Garvie," she said. "Can the theme be animals? We've never had that one before."

Mrs. Garvie smiled. "Animals!" she said. "I might have known that's what you'd come up with. It sounds like a terrific idea, Mandy."

Mandy blushed and James clapped her on the back.

"Great idea," he said.

"What do the rest of you think?" asked Mrs. Garvie.

There was a general murmur of approval from the rest of the pupils.

"I think it sounds terrific," said Peter Foster. "Can I bring Timmy?"

Mrs. Garvie gave him a look. "As long as you don't let him off the leash, Peter," she said. "We all know the mischief Timmy can get into."

"Can we have a go-cart race at the picnic?" Andrew Pearson said. "Beacon Hill is great for go-carts."

Andrew was in Mandy's class. His older brother had helped him make a go-cart last year. It started a craze and now a lot of kids in the village had go-carts. James had been talking about getting his dad to help him make one.

Mrs. Garvie looked doubtful.

"That depends, Andrew," she said. "How many people have go-carts?"

Half a dozen hands shot up into the air, Peter's among them.

"Pam Stanton's got one," said Mandy, looking across to where Pam was waving her hand wildly in the air.

"I wish I had a go-cart," James said. "I'd love to enter the race."

Mandy looked at him. "I thought your dad was going to help you make one," she said.

James nodded. "He is," he said. "But we haven't gotten around to it yet. Dad's been really busy at work. He hasn't had time."

"I could help you," Mandy said.

James smiled. "Thanks, Mandy," he said. "But I wouldn't even know where to start. And Dad says if I have a go-cart it has to be safe."

Mrs. Garvie counted the raised hands.

"Oh, well," she said. "That's plenty of competition for a race. I think we can have a go-cart race."

"What's that got to do with animals?" Jill Redfern said.

"We can give the go-carts animal names," said Andrew.

Jill grinned. "Peter can call his the *Terrier*," she said.

"Lucky for you, Jill, you haven't got a go-cart," said Peter. "You'd have to call it the *Tortoise*."

Jill stuck out her tongue. She had a pet tortoise called Toto.

Mrs. Garvie coughed and gave them a look.

"Sorry, Mrs. Garvie," said Jill.

"But Andrew's idea is a good one," said

Mandy. "We can have all kinds of animal races. Like hedgehog races where you have to roll."

"And snake races where you have to slither," said Jill.

"I'll bring Gertie," said Gary Roberts. "She can show you how it's done."

Gary Roberts had a pet garter snake called Gertie.

"Can we have a rabbit race?" piped up a voice.

Mrs. Garvie looked down at little Laura Baker.

"Of course we can, Laura," she said. "You ask Mandy about it later."

Mandy turned to James. "We could use sacks for the rabbit race, so that people would have to hop," she said.

"What?" said James, and Mandy knew he was still thinking about the go-cart race.

Mrs. Garvie looked at the assembled students. "You've got a lot to think about," she said. "Let Mandy have your ideas and don't forget we'll need a name for the day as well."

They always had a name for the picnic day. Last year it had been Pirate Playtime.

"Animal Antics!" said James and then blushed. James didn't usually call out during assembly.

People liked the name and began repeating it as they filed out of the assembly hall.

"Animal Antics," said Mandy to James as they separated to go to their classrooms. "That's a terrific name."

James looked pleased. But he still wasn't as cheerful as usual. Mandy watched as he walked away down the corridor, wondering how she could help.

"Mandy, Mandy can we really have a rabbit race?" said a voice at Mandy's elbow.

Mandy turned and looked down at Laura Baker. Laura was seven years old. She had dark curly hair tied up on top of her head with a big red bow. Jack Gardiner was with her.

"Hi, Laura. Hello, Jack," Mandy said. "Sure we'll have a rabbit race, Laura. How is Fluffy? Has she had her babies yet?"

Laura beamed. "Not yet," she said. "But she's fine. It won't be long now."

Mandy looked at Jack. The little boy looked terribly unhappy.

"How are you doing, Jack?" she asked.

Jack looked up at her. "Okay," he said in a dull voice.

"I'm supposed to look after him," said Laura importantly. "He's in my class and he's going to sit next to me."

Mandy smiled at the little girl. "I'm sure you'll look after him very well, Laura," she said.

"Come on, Jack," said Laura. "We'd better hurry or we'll be late." And Laura sped off down the corridor.

Mandy looked at Jack. Then she looked around. Everybody else had gone.

"Look, Jack," she said quietly. "I heard about Fred."

Jack's big blue eyes filled with tears.

Mandy put out a hand and touched his shoulder.

"Wouldn't you like another pet?" she said.

Jack looked up at her and blinked the tears away.

"I'll never have another pet," he said. "And I'll never like living here."

Mandy looked at him sadly. She understood how lonely he felt. Suddenly a voice called down the corridor.

"Hurry up, Jack!" Laura yelled. "You don't want to be late on your very first day."

Jack turned and marched away. Mandy sighed. First James and now Jack. What was she going to do about them?

4

A Surprise for James

Mandy sat at the kitchen table in Lilac Cottage on Tuesday afternoon, swinging her legs and thinking.

"And how is little Jack Gardiner doing at school?" asked Mandy's grandma.

"How did you know I was thinking about Jack?" Mandy said.

Grandma's eyes twinkled. "Magic!" she said.

Mandy grinned, then she looked serious. "I tried to cheer him up," she said. "But he just doesn't seem to *want* to like Welford."

"What about him getting another pet?" said Grandma.

Mandy shook her head. "He doesn't want to hear about it," she said.

"Perhaps it's just too soon," said Grandma.

"Maybe," Mandy said doubtfully. "But don't you think if he had a pet to look after he would feel so much better?"

Grandma smiled. "I'm sure you're right," she said. "Now cheer up and drink your orange juice. I've got work to do in the garage and you can help me."

Mandy raised her glass to her mouth and finished her drink.

"There," she said, wiping her mouth. "That was yummy. And those chocolate cookies! You really *are* magic, Grandma."

"My special recipe," said Grandma, opening

the kitchen door. "But you still don't look very cheerful."

"Oh, I've got another problem," said Mandy as she followed her grandma down the path to the garage.

"What's that?" said a voice from the garage. "Did you say you had a problem, Mandy?"

Mandy peered into the garage. Dust danced in the sunlight in the doorway. She shaded her eyes.

"Is that you, Grandpa?" she said.

Grandpa poked his head out from behind a pile of boxes.

"It certainly is," he said. "In here up to my ears in junk."

"That isn't junk, that's just disorganized," said Grandma.

Grandpa looked at her and pushed his hat back on his head. "It's disorganized to you, Dorothy," he said. "But it's junk to me. Look at this."

He pulled a carriage out from behind an old dresser.

Grandma looked at it. "Well, maybe you're right about that," she said. "It *is* rather old."

Grandpa let out a whoop of laughter. "Rather old?" he said. "It was Mandy's carriage. Look at it! It's falling apart."

Mandy looked at the carriage. "I can't imagine I was ever little enough to fit in there," she said.

Grandpa grinned. "You weren't too little to wreck it," he said. "You never did like being strapped into a carriage, Mandy."

"Don't listen to him, Mandy," Grandma said. "You were a lively baby, that's all."

Grandpa chuckled. "That's one way of putting it," he said.

"The wheels are all right," Mandy said, examining the carriage.

Grandpa looked at them. "I remember when your dad was a boy," he said, turning to push the carriage out of the way. "I showed him how to make a fine go-cart out of a set of old carriage wheels and a couple of wooden boxes."

Mandy's head shot up. "What?" she said. "What did you say, Grandpa?"

Grandpa looked at her in surprise. "What's the matter?" he said.

Mandy was nearly dancing with excitement. "Could you do it again?" she said. "Could you make another go-cart?"

Grandpa scratched his head. "I believe I could," he said, looking puzzled. "I didn't know you wanted a go-cart."

Mandy shook her head. "Not for me," she said. "For James." And she told Grandma and Grandpa all about the go-cart race.

Grandpa smiled when she finished.

"Tell you what," he said. "You and James collect all the things we need and I'll help you make the best go-cart in Welford."

"What kind of things do you need?" asked Mandy.

Grandpa thought for a moment. "A couple of strong wooden boxes," he said. "Or, better still, some fresh wood. I've got sandpaper, but we'd need some paint. We've got the wheels."

He looked at Mandy's old carriage. "And I think we could use the bottom of the carriage to make the base. It's a good, solid one. I might even be able to fit the brake to the go-cart."

"What about my old bike?" said Mandy. "It's got brakes."

"That might do," said Grandpa. "Then all we'd need is a guide rope. It's amazing what you can make out of a few bits and pieces. I used to build some great go-carts when I was a boy."

"And you'll help James?" said Mandy.

Grandpa laughed. "I'd love to," he said. "It'll be just like old times. I can hardly wait for the two of you to collect the stuff."

Mandy shook her head. "Oh, I'll collect all the stuff myself," she said. "I want it to be a surprise for James. Just wait until I present him with everything he needs! What do you think he'll say?" She looked at her grandma and grandpa. "You know what," she said. "You're *both* magic!"

She grinned up at Grandma and Grandpa.

That was one of her problems solved. Now all she had to do was solve the other one.

Mandy was so deep in thought as she cycled past Hobart's Corner that she didn't notice the small figure sitting on the garden wall.

"Wood, rope, paint," she muttered to herself.

"Hello," said Jack.

Mandy looked up, surprised. "Oh, hello, Jack," she said, coming to a stop. "I didn't see you there."

"You were talking to yourself," said Jack.

Mandy smiled at him. This was the first time he had spoken to her first.

"Can you keep a secret?" she asked.

Jack's eyes lit up with interest for a moment. "What kind of a secret?" he said.

"The surprise kind," she said. And she told him about the go-cart for James.

"That sounds great," said Jack, his eyes shining.

Mandy was amazed. For the first time she saw him happy. He looked like a different person.

"So now I'm going to go around the village collecting everything I need," she said.

"Where are you going to look?" said Jack.

Mandy thought for a moment. "I can get wood from Amy Fenton's dad at the lumberyard," she said. "Then I thought I might try Laura's dad for nails. He was making a nesting box for Fluffy last week so he must have some."

"Fluffy?" said Jack.

"One of Laura's rabbits," said Mandy. "She

must have told you about Fluffy. She's going to have babies soon."

Jack nodded. "Yes, she did," he said, kicking at the garden wall.

Mandy stopped as an idea suddenly occurred to her. All of the people she planned to visit had pets.

She looked at Jack. He wasn't interested in another pet. But what if he *saw* some pets? He might change his mind. It was worth a try.

"Of course all this stuff is going to be awfully heavy," she said with a sigh. "I don't know how I'm going to manage it all on my own."

Jack looked at her. She could see him trying to make up his mind.

"Do you want some help?" he said at last.

Mandy smiled. "Oh, Jack, that would be great," she said. "Would your mom let you?"

"I'll ask her," said Jack. "When do you want to go?"

Mandy bit her lip. She didn't want to give Jack a chance to change his mind.

"Now," she said firmly. "Everyone will be at home.

"Okay," said Jack. "I'll run and ask Mom."

Mandy hugged herself, crossed her fingers, and turned around three times for good luck until Jack got back. If her plan worked, Jack might — just might — be back tonight asking his mom another favor.

"I've got to be home by six," Jack said as he came running back to the gate, pushing his bike.

Mandy beamed at him. "No problem," she said. "We should have everything by then."

5

Visiting

Mandy and Jack's first call was at Amy Fenton's house.

"Amy's dad runs the lumberyard on Walton Road," Mandy said as she and Jack cycled up Main Street. "That's a good place to start if we're looking for wood."

Jack nodded. "Amy Fenton," he said. "I haven't met her. Is she in your class?"

"She's in James's class," Mandy replied. She took a quick sideways look at him. "She's got a pet mouse named Minnie."

Jack cycled on, his eyes straight ahead.

"Here we are," Mandy said. "And there's Amy in the garden."

She braked and leaped off her bike, waving to Amy.

"Amy," she called. "We've got a really big favor to ask."

Mandy explained what she and Jack were looking for, and Amy said she would ask her dad if he could help.

"Come and see Minnie while you're waiting," she said.

Mandy smiled. She hadn't even had to ask.

"You'll love Minnie," Mandy said to Jack as Amy took them into her bedroom and went off to get her dad.

Jack looked at the little white mouse in its

cage. It pushed its tiny pink nose up against the bars, twitching its whiskers and looking at them with bright eyes.

Mandy gently opened the cage and took Minnie out, letting her run up and down her arm.

"You hold her, Jack," she said.

But Jack shook his head. "I think Amy's coming back," he said, turning away.

Mandy sighed. It wasn't going to be easy getting Jack interested in another pet.

"Great news," said Amy, coming into the room. "Dad says he can let you have some scraps. He'll deliver them to Lilac Cottage tomorrow if that's all right."

"Terrific!" said Mandy. She giggled as Minnie scampered up her arm and tickled the back of her neck.

"And Mom says Aunt Julia has loads of old cans of paint lying around in her garden shed," Amy finished.

"Even better," Mandy said. "We'll go there right now."

Mandy sighed. Amy's Aunt Julia was Richard Tanner's mom. And Richard Tanner had a Persian cat named Duchess. If Jack didn't like mice, maybe he would like cats better.

But Jack didn't seem to like Duchess any more than he had liked Minnie. The Persian cat stalked through the garden in front of them as they made their way out to the shed.

"Isn't she beautiful?" said Mandy, bending to stroke the cat's long, silky fur.

Jack stretched out a hand to Duchess but the

cat must have sensed his reluctance. She backed away from him. Jack drew his hand back quickly.

"She won't hurt you," Richard said.

"I don't like cats much anyway," said Jack.

Richard nodded. "That must be it," he said. "Cats know when people don't like them."

Mandy sighed as she watched Duchess flick her tail and disappear behind the garden shed. But they *did* come away with four half full cans of paint.

The next house they tried was where Gary Roberts lived. Gary wanted to be an inventor when he grew up, so his bedroom was always full of junk — or so his mom said.

"I bet Gary has something useful," said Mandy.

While Gary searched through his bedroom closet, Jack inspected Gary's garter snake, Gertie. Mandy held her breath. He looked really interested. Gertie slithered toward him, her green and yellow body gleaming. She raised her head slightly, her tongue flicking in and out. Jack and Gertie stared at each other. Maybe Jack would like a *snake*, Mandy thought.

"I knew I had one of these somewhere," Gary yelled from the depths of the closet.

There was a honking sound and Jack spun around, forgetting about Gertie.

Mandy put the snake back in her tank and looked at the rusty, old-fashioned motorcar horn in Gary's hand.

"Oh, thanks, Gary," she said. "That's going to be really useful."

Jack took the horn and turned it around. The rubber bulb was almost worn through in places and the metal clip was rusted.

"This is great," he said grinning at Mandy.

"Don't mention it," Gary said. "Any time! Now I thought I had a steering wheel in here somewhere."

"Don't bother, Gary," Mandy said hastily. "The horn is enough."

Mandy packed the horn into her bicycle basket alongside the cans of paint.

"What else do we need?" said Jack.

Mandy looked at her list. "Rope," she said. "I wonder where we could get that?"

"I could chop a bit off Mom's clothesline," said Jack.

Mandy gave him a look. "And get into trouble?" She smiled. Even if she wasn't being very successful with this pet idea, Jack was certainly friendlier than he had been before.

"I know," he said. "Laura said she got a new jump rope yesterday. Maybe she would let us have her old one."

"Good idea," said Mandy. "Let's go."

Laura met them at the door, her face flushed with excitement.

"Oh, you'll never guess," she said. "Fluffy is having her kittens — right now!"

"Now?" Mandy breathed. "Oh, Laura, that's wonderful. How is she? How many kittens are there so far?"

"Kittens?" said Jack, puzzled.

"That's what you call baby rabbits," Laura said. "Come and see. But don't make a noise.

Fluffy has been in a hutch on her own since she got pregnant and she's used to everything being really quiet."

Mandy and Jack followed Laura through to the greenhouse where Mr. Baker had set up a separate hutch for Fluffy. Pregnant rabbits had to be on their own because, as well as needing extra feeding, they had to start nest-building. And they couldn't do that in a hutch with other rabbits.

Mrs. Baker was already there, kneeling down in front of the hutch. She put her fingers to her lips as the children came in.

Mandy and Jack crouched down with Laura between them and gazed at the black-and-white doe. The nesting box was inside the hutch. It was a simple open-sided box with fresh hay bedding. Mandy could see that it was lined with soft fur. She knew that Fluffy would have plucked fur from her belly to line the box so that her babies would have a soft bed to lie on.

Then Mandy forgot everything else as she

caught sight of Fluffy's babies — tiny, furry little things. They lay there, snuggled into Fluffy's
body, their eyes tightly closed.

"Ugh!" said Jack. "They're all wet!"

"Sshh!" Laura whispered. "If you disturb her
she might get frightened and she might eat her
babies. We must be very quiet."

Mandy held her breath as Fluffy stretched
and began to breathe more heavily. Her huge
dark eyes rolled toward Mandy as she strained
to give birth.

"Come on, Fluffy," Mandy whispered under her breath. "Good girl, you can do it."

Then there was another baby, and another. At last, Fluffy relaxed.

"Five," Laura whispered as Fluffy bent her head to her babies. "Do you think she's finished?"

Mrs. Baker nodded. "It looks like it," she said quietly. "Look at the way she is licking her kittens now."

Laura turned a shining face to Mandy and Jack. "Oh, wasn't that wonderful?" she said. "And all her babies look just fine."

Jack was looking at Fluffy and her babies, his face lit up in a way Mandy had never seen before.

"Oh," she said. "Wasn't that the best thing you ever saw? Look at the little rabbits. They're so tiny and helpless."

"They can't see or hear yet," said Laura. "Their eyes won't open for another ten days."

Mrs. Baker smiled. "They've got their mother to look after them for the next two months. They'll depend on her for milk," she said. "After that we'll have to find homes for them."

Jack turned to her. "But who will you give them to?" he said.

"To people who will love them and care for them," Mrs. Baker said. "Maybe even someone like you."

"Me?" said Jack as if he couldn't believe it. "You mean I could have one of Fluffy's babies?"

Mandy looked at Jack, her eyes shining. Mrs. Baker examined Jack's eager face.

"Oh, please, Mommy," said Laura. "I can tell Jack all about taking care of rabbits."

"Are you used to taking care of a pet, Jack?" Mrs. Baker said. "They can be a lot of work, you know."

Jack flushed and Mandy held her breath.

"I used to have a dog," he said. "But he died. I'd like another pet now."

Mrs. Baker looked from Jack to Laura to Mandy.

"I just know Jack would love his pet," Mandy said.

Mrs. Baker smiled. "Then why don't you ask your parents?" she said to Jack. "If they say yes, then you can be the first to choose, Jack. You can have the pick of Fluffy's litter."

Jack's face blazed with happiness. "I'd like that," he said. "I'd like that a lot."

Mandy felt the smile spreading over her own face. Success!

When they got back to Hobart's Corner, Mrs. Gardiner was just coming out of the kitchen door into the garden. Jack skidded his bike to a halt and raced across to her.

"Mom, Mom!" he yelled as he ran. "Laura says I can have one of Fluffy's baby rabbits if you'll let me." He stopped in front of his mother, looking up at her.

"A baby rabbit?" Mrs. Gardiner said. "A new pet?"

Jack bit his lip. "I know you're really busy, but it wouldn't be any trouble," he said. "It's just a *little* rabbit."

Mrs. Gardiner smiled. "I think we could manage to give a little rabbit a home," she said. "As long as you promise to look after it."

Jack's face lit up. "Oh, I will, Mom," he said. "So can I really have a rabbit as a pet?"

Mrs. Gardiner looked across the top of Jack's head at Mandy. Then she crouched down in front of Jack and put her arms around him.

"Of course you can, Jack," she said. She looked into Mandy's eyes, smiling. "I think that's a wonderful idea."

6

Getting Ready

The following afternoon Mandy, Grandma, Grandpa, and James were standing in the driveway of Lilac Cottage. Blackie was busy wrapping his leash around James's ankles. James had his eyes shut.

"Okay, you can open your eyes now," Mandy said to James.

James opened his eyes and looked at the pile of things on the floor of the garage.

Blackie pulled at his leash and sniffed at a can of black paint.

Then he sneezed and shook himself.

"What's all this?" said James.

"Guess!" said Mandy.

James looked puzzled. "It looks like a heap of junk to me," he said.

Mandy put her hands on her hips and looked at him. "Well, James Hunter," she said, "it might look like a pile of old junk to you *now*, but once you and Grandpa have finished with it, it's going to be the best go-cart in Welford. At least that's what Grandpa says." And she turned to look at her grandpa.

"That's right," said Grandpa.

James was standing there with his mouth open. "A go-cart?" he said. "You mean we're going to make one?"

Mandy laughed. "Not me! Grandpa's the expert," she said.

"But you're going to help," Grandpa said to James.

James turned to him, his face shining. "Oh, Mr. Hope, this is terrific." He looked at Mandy. "Where did you get all this stuff?"

"Oh, here and there," said Mandy. "And I've got more news for you. Jack wants one of Laura's baby rabbits."

"No kidding," said James. "How did you manage that?"

Grandma smiled. "Come inside and get a cold drink and Mandy can tell you all about it," she said.

"And then we'll draw up the plans for the go-cart," Grandpa said.

"Oh, and Grandpa," said Mandy, "could you please help Jack make a rabbit hutch? There's plenty of wood here. Jack's mom and dad are so busy with all the work at Hobart's Corner they won't have time."

Grandpa pushed his hat back and scratched his head. "And I thought I was supposed to be retired," he said. He looked at James. "Come on, boy," he said. "Let's have our break before the whole of Welford starts lining up for carpentry work!"

James looked at Blackie. "But what about Blackie?" he said. "We were going to have a training session this afternoon."

Mandy took Blackie's leash. "Just leave Blackie to us," she said. "Grandma and I are going to train him."

James laughed. "Do you hear that, Blackie?" he said. "You'd better be on your best behavior."

Blackie looked up at him and put his head to one side.

"And don't try looking pathetic," Grandma said to the little animal. "It's all for your own good."

Blackie lay down, put his head on his paws, and sighed.

Grandma shook her head. "That puppy might not be the most obedient dog in the world," she said. "But I swear he understands every word you say to him."

"Biscuit!" Mandy said to Blackie.

The puppy was up on his feet at once, trotting beside her, tail wagging.

"It looks as if you're right, Grandma," she said. "Now all we've got to do is to try and get him to do the things he *doesn't* want to do."

Grandpa and James spent the next week working on the go-cart. James couldn't talk about anything else.

"Your grandpa taught me how to use a saw," he said proudly on the way to school one morning. "And he showed me how to cut dovetailed joints."

"What are they?" Mandy asked.

James tried to explain but Mandy couldn't follow him.

"Come and see it," said James. "It's looking really great."

So, that evening, Mandy went to Lilac Cottage with James.

"Wow!" she said when Grandpa wheeled the

go-cart out of the garage. "That looks great. Are those really my old carriage wheels?"

Grandpa smiled. "They look a bit different now, don't they?" he said.

"You can say that again," said Mandy, staring at the long, low wooden structure perched on its wheels.

James ran his hand over the smooth wood of the go-cart. "Those are dovetailed joints," he said, pointing to the deep box seat at the back of the go-cart.

Mandy looked closely. The side of the seat was joined to the back almost like a jigsaw.

"Now we have to attach a footboard and guide rope to the front," said James.

"A what?" said Mandy.

"It's a bit like a steering wheel," said Grandpa. "Or a tiller on a boat."

"Oh, right," said Mandy. She grinned. "Tell you what," she said. "I think this is going to knock spots off Andrew's go-cart."

"You bet!" said James.

Grandpa looked at him. "Ready?" he said.

"We've still got a long way to go if this is going to be the best go-cart in Welford."

James picked up a hammer and a handful of nails. "You bet!" he said again, laughing.

After that, Mandy went to Lilac Cottage every evening. She was soon involved in helping with the go-cart — and Jack's rabbit hutch.

The rabbit hutch was coming along, but a little slower than the go-cart. Grandpa had built a sturdy frame on legs. It stood about a foot off the ground. Grandpa was letting Jack do as much as he could and Mandy could see that Jack was loving it. Each evening after dinner he raced straight to Lilac Cottage to work on the cage.

Jack liked carpentry as much as James did, but Grandpa liked someone to keep a close eye on him. So Mandy soon got into the habit of working with Jack.

With Grandpa's help, they had glued and nailed the sides of the rabbit cage together. Then they fitted the partition between the two compartments inside the cage, and, finally, got ready to attach the roof to the sides.

"The roof has to overhang the cage," Grandpa said. "You don't want the rain to get in — or cats, either."

"Would cats hurt a rabbit?" Jack asked.

Grandpa took a roll of chicken wire and measured a length off it against the front of the hutch. "A cat would kill a baby rabbit," he said. Then he looked at Jack's concerned face. "But we're going to make your hutch cat-proof!"

7

The Cheetah

Two days later, James's go-cart was almost finished.

"There," James said proudly from the driveway. "It just needs some paint now. What do you think of the go-cart, Mandy?"

Blackie gave a short bark and leaped up at James's chest.

"Sit!" said Mandy and to her surprise, Blackie sat and looked up at her.

Mandy gave him a pat, making a fuss over him for being a good dog, and looked at the go-cart. It sat outside the garage at Lilac Cottage, the spokes of its wheels polished and sparkling in the sun. "It's terrific!" she said.

James beamed and even Grandpa looked proud.

"I'm pretty pleased with it myself," he said, looking at the finished product. There was an open box mounted on the back with a seat built into it. Mandy looked at the long piece of wood with a crossbar on the end that stretched from below the seat to the front of the go-cart.

"What's that?" she said.

James got into the go-cart and sat on the seat

"It's for steering," he said, putting his feet on the crossbar and pushing. "It's like a kind of rudder."

Mandy watched as the front wheels turned from side to side.

James picked up the looped rope that was lying across the front of the go-cart.

"And that's the guide rope," Grandpa said. "James can control the go-cart with his feet and his hands."

"Wow!" said Mandy. "You're a genius, Grandpa."

Grandpa laughed. "You're a bit of a genius yourself," he said, looking down at Blackie, who was sitting quietly by Mandy's feet. "You've certainly got Blackie well on the way to being the model puppy."

Mandy laughed. "Grandma's the one who's really good with him," she said. She turned to James. "What animal are you going to name your go-cart after?" she said.

James stuck a hand in his back pocket and pulled out a picture he had cut out of a magazine. It was a very large cat with a reddish-yellow coat broken up by solid black spots. There were stripes running from the corner of its eyes down the sides of its nose.

"It's a cheetah," she said.

James nodded. "Did you know that the cheetah is the fastest animal in the world?" he said. "There are records of them running at speeds of up to sixty-eight miles per hour. So, if I've got the fastest go-cart, it ought to be named after the fastest animal."

"We can paint it in cheetah colors," said Mandy. "I've got some black paint and we can mix red and yellow to get the base color. James, your go-cart is going to be the nicest one in Welford."

Grandpa pointed to the cans of paint piled up at the side of the garage.

"Paint and brushes," he said. "You two better get started."

The gate at the back garden opened and Mandy looked up. Jack was coming up the path with his mother.

"And here's my other apprentice carpenter," Grandpa said smiling. "Hello, Mrs. Gardiner. How are you settling in?"

Mrs. Gardiner came up the path toward them. "I think we're getting there," she said.

"But there's so much work to do. I just came to thank you all for all your help building this hutch with Jack."

Mandy grinned. "Grandpa is loving it," she said. "Aren't you, Grandpa?"

Mr. Hope laughed. "I certainly am," he said. "Your Jack is going to turn into a fine carpenter."

Jack beamed with pride as Mandy turned to him.

"Hi, Jack!" she said. "Where have you been? You look like you've got good news."

"Hoppy opened his eyes today," he said excitedly. "I've just been to see him!"

"Hoppy?" said James.

Jack nodded. "That's what I'm going to call my rabbit," he said.

"Great!" said Mandy. "What color is he?"

"Black and white," Jack said. "Just like his mom."

Grandpa looked at Jack. "We'd better finish this hutch then, Jack," he said. "We want to have it ready in good time."

Jack nodded. "But it'll be another six weeks before I can take Hoppy home," he said. "He's only two weeks old. He still needs his mother to feed him."

"He'll soon be on solid food," said Mrs. Gardiner. "Then *you* can feed him."

"Laura says we can start giving him some solids when he's three or four weeks old," said Jack. "I can't wait to try feeding him. And I can't wait to take him home."

"Then let's get busy," said Grandpa. "We want this hutch to be fit for a king."

"Oh, we do," said Jack. "We really do!" Mrs. Gardiner looked at him. "He's a different boy these days," she said to Grandpa. "You and your wife have been so kind."

"It's a pleasure," Grandpa said. "Why don't you go in and have a word with Dorothy?" His eyes twinkled. "And if she's putting the kettle on for a cup of tea, I wouldn't say no."

Mrs. Gardiner laughed and walked toward the house. "I'll tell her," she said.

"Right," said Mandy, rolling up her sleeves. "I'll give James a hand with the go-cart."

When Mandy and James finished painting the go-cart it looked even better. They stood back and admired it.

"Those black markings look really good," said Mandy. She looked at the picture of the cheetah James had pinned to the garage wall. "Just like the real thing," she said.

James turned to look, too. Then something ran between them both, whizzing around the paint cans. Mandy saw the yellow paint can rock slightly, then it tumbled over, spreading a pool of paint over the garage floor.

"Blackie!" James shouted.

The puppy stopped abruptly, turned around, skidded on the wet paint, and rolled over.

"Oh, no!" said Mandy. Then she started to laugh.

"What are you laughing for?" said James as Blackie scooted off across the garden.

"Look!" said Mandy, pointing. Blackie's coat

was patterned black and yellow all over. "He's like a miniature cheetah."

James shook his head. "How on earth are we going to get that paint out of his coat?"

Mandy bit her lip to stop laughing. "We'll ask Mom and Dad," she said. "They'll know what to do."

"Paint remover," said Jack, turning around from the hutch. He looked a little sad for a moment. "Fred once got red paint all over him. We got it off with paint remover and then gave him a good shampoo."

"Just make sure you don't get any of the fluid in his eyes," said Grandpa. "There's a bottle of it on the shelf here."

"Thanks for the tip, Jack," James said. "I'll just see if I can catch him."

Mandy walked over to Jack and the rabbit hutch. Grandpa and Jack had just finished nailing chicken wire onto one side of the hutch.

"I'll help you with the hutch again tomorrow," she said. "There isn't much to do now, is there?"

"We still have to make the doors — one solid and one with wire mesh for each part of the hutch," said Grandpa. He looked at Jack. "But I've got a great little helper here."

Jack flushed with pride again. "Hoppy is going to love this hutch," he said. "I was in the pet shop in Walton yesterday. The owner showed me this special drinking bottle with a tube on the end. You fix it to the outside of the cage and then the water stays clean. I'm saving up for one."

Mandy examined the hutch. What a perfect

75

home it was going to be for Jack's rabbit. She smiled to herself as Jack talked eagerly about Hoppy and his hutch. Jack had certainly changed since Hoppy had come into his life.

8

Hoppy's New Home

"Breakfast!" Dr. Emily called.

Mandy raced downstairs and into the kitchen at Animal Ark. Dr. Emily turned from the stove and put a dish of fluffy scrambled eggs on the table just as Dr. Adam came through the door.

"That looks good," he said, helping himself.

Dr. Emily put down a plate of toast and the teapot and settled herself at the table. Mandy looked around the room. She loved the kitchen at Animal Ark with its old oak beams and the copper pans hanging down from them. The red check curtains at the open window fluttered in the summer breeze. Mandy sighed with contentment.

"You look happy," Dr. Adam said with a smile.

Mandy nodded. "I'm going to Laura's with Jack today to pick up his rabbit."

Dr. Emily poured the tea and looked at Mandy. "How are you getting the rabbit back to Jack's house?" she asked.

"I thought I would borrow a small animal carrier from here," Mandy said. "If that's okay?"

Her father chewed thoughtfully on a piece of toast. "Make sure you line it with some of the bedding from Fluffy's hutch," he said. "Rabbits have a very good sense of smell. If the new hutch smells familiar, the baby rabbit will settle more quickly.

"I will," said Mandy. "Thanks, Dad!" She looked at her watch. "I'd better go. Jack will be waiting."

"Have a good time," said Dr. Emily.

Mandy's face was shining. "Oh, I will," she said. "Jack is so excited. Grandpa was taking the hutch over to help him set it up first thing this morning. I hope everything went okay."

Jack was waiting for her at the front gate when she got to Laura's. She looked at the little boy's excited face. "Come on," Mandy said, opening the gate. "Let's go and get him."

"He's all ready," Laura said as she opened the door to them. "I told him you were coming for him today."

She led the way through the hall and out of the back door into garden. "There," she said.

Jack walked slowly toward the hutch. Fluffy looked up, her nose twitching.

"Hello, Fluffy," Mandy said, bending close to the hutch and putting a finger through the mesh.

Fluffy wiggled her ears and sniffed at Mandy's outstretched finger. There were two baby rabbits in the hutch with her. They were both black and white like their mother. Mandy hadn't seen the baby rabbits since they had left the nesting box but she knew Jack had been to see Hoppy nearly every day. Jack and Laura were great friends now.

"Where are all the rest of the babies?" Mandy said.

Laura sighed. "Mom said I could only keep one for myself," she said. "We found homes for all the others."

She opened the hutch door and picked one of the baby rabbits up very gently.

"Look," she said. "I chose this one. I'm going to call him Patch."

"Was it easy finding homes for all the rest?" said Mandy.

Laura nodded. "Oh, yes," she said. "Once

Jack started telling people about Hoppy, every-body wanted one."

Mandy looked at Jack. No wonder she hadn't seen so much of him at school recently. He was obviously making friends — and that was even before he'd brought Hoppy home.

Mandy opened the carrier box she had brought. She scooped some of the old bedding out of Fluffy's hutch and spread it in among the clean newspapers in the bottom of the carrier.

"Dad says the smell of Fluffy's bedding will help Hoppy to settle down better," she said.

Laura nodded and put Patch back into the hutch.

"There, Fluffy," she said. "You take care of Patch." She gave Fluffy a pat. "She's so thin and her coat looks really dull."

"That's only because she's used up all her energy feeding her babies," Mandy said. "She'll be back to normal soon."

"That's what Mom says," said Laura. "But I still feel sorry for her. Especially since she's had to say good-bye to all her babies — except

Patch." She turned to Jack. "Do you want to take Hoppy out?"

Jack nodded and moved toward the hutch. "How do I pick him up?" he said.

"Just like I did," said Laura. "He's small enough to sit in your hand. But when he grows bigger you'll have to pick him up by the scruff of the neck."

Jack looked alarmed.

"It's easy," said Laura. "And it doesn't hurt the rabbit. Look!" She reached into the hutch and picked up Fluffy, holding onto the fur at the back of the rabbit's neck with one hand and supporting her bottom with the other.

Jack reached into the hutch and gathered Hoppy gently into his hands. "This is easier," he said.

Mandy smiled. "Well done, Jack," she said as he carried Hoppy over to the carrier. "And if you let him lie along your arm with his head snuggled into the crook of your elbow, he'll let you carry him quite happily."

Jack laid the little rabbit along his arm.

Hoppy looked up at him with big dark eyes. "He doesn't reach the crook of my elbow," he said, laughing.

"Not yet," Mandy said. "But rabbits grow fast."

Hoppy pushed against Jack's arm with his back legs. "Look at that," said Jack. "He's really strong already."

"That's why rabbits are so good at hopping," Laura said. "They have such strong back legs."

Mandy stroked Hoppy's black and white coat gently and the little animal settled down.

Laura turned to Mandy. "I can't wait for the picnic," she said. "I'm really looking forward to the rabbit race."

"The rabbit race," said Jack, looking thoughtful. "You'd like that, wouldn't you, Hoppy?"

Jack put the little rabbit gently into the carrier. Hoppy began snuffling around, twitching his nose and sniffing at the bedding.

"I can't wait to get him home," said Jack. "Do you think he'll like his new hutch?"

"After all the work you and Grandpa put into it?" Mandy said. "He'll love it! Just you wait and see."

"Oh, Jack, that's perfect!" Mandy said when she saw the hutch in Jack's garden.

The hutch stood about a foot off the ground on sturdy wooden legs, well out of reach of cats. It was placed in the angle of a south-facing wall, just where the kitchen joined the main house.

"Do you think it'll be all right there?" Jack asked anxiously. "Your grandpa thought that was the right place."

Mandy smiled at him. "Of course it will," she said. "No drafts and it'll get lots of sunshine." She laid her hand on the shingle-covered roof. It stuck out beyond the front of the hutch so that no rain could get in. Grandpa had thought of everything. "And that's perfect, too," she said. "Hoppy will be warm and dry in there."

The kitchen door opened and Mrs. Gardiner

looked out. She was wearing a pair of baggy, paint-stained jeans and her hair was tied up in a bright blue scarf.

"Oh, you're back," she said to Jack. "Hello, Mandy." Then she caught sight of Hoppy. "Oh, isn't he gorgeous!" she said.

"Beautiful," Mandy said, looking at Hoppy. The little rabbit was sitting back on his haunches washing his ears.

There was a call from inside the house and Mrs. Gardiner looked around.

Coming," she called back. She looked at Mandy. "I don't think this house will ever be ready," she said. "And I've got the first guests booked for the end of the month." She drew a hand over her forehead. "Can you fix yourselves some drinks? There's orange juice in the refrigerator."

Mandy nodded. "Once we've got Hoppy bedded down," she said.

Jack smiled. "Animals first," he said.

"If you need some food for Hoppy, help yourselves out of the vegetable basket," Mrs.

Gardiner said as she disappeared back into the house.

Mandy and Jack looked at each other.

"What now?" said Jack.

"First the bedding," Mandy said. "Then food and water."

"Right," said Jack. "Come and see what I've got."

Jack had collected a whole pile of old newspapers.

"Mom and I divided them up," he said. "She needed lots to cover the floor while they're decorating."

"These are great," said Mandy. "We should put four or five layers of newspaper in the bottom of the hutch."

"And I've got lots of sawdust and wood shavings," said Jack, opening a black plastic bag. He grinned. "Dad's been doing a lot of sawing and I got some from your grandpa, too."

Mandy finished laying the newspapers in the hutch and scooped up a few handfuls of shavings and sawdust. She covered the newspapers with the mixture and smoothed it out.

"That should do," she said, looking at it. "Now, what else do we need?"

"Straw," said Jack. "For Hoppy's bedroom."

Jack opened another bag and pulled out some straw. It smelled sweet and fresh. He unlatched the wooden door of the sleeping compartment and spread the straw out on the floor. "There," he said. "Now all we need are food and water and we can put Hoppy in."

Jack disappeared into the kitchen and came out carrying a box of rabbit cereal mix and a heavy blue dog bowl.

"This was Fred's bowl," he said. His bottom lip trembled a little.

Mandy looked at the bowl. "It's very nice," she said gently. "And I'm sure Fred would be glad that it's Hoppy's now."

Jack nodded. "He would, wouldn't he?" he said. Mandy saw him blink some tears away. Then he placed the bowl firmly inside the hutch. "It's yours now, Hoppy," he said. Then he started opening the cereal packet. "You're going to like this."

Mandy gave a little sigh of relief. Jack would never forget Fred, but it looked as if he would get over his sadness with Hoppy to care for.

"What about water?" she asked as Jack poured cereal into the bowl.

"I bought one of those plastic bottles," said Jack.

Mandy nodded. "They're good," she said. "The water doesn't get dirty or spilled."

Soon they had the hutch ready. Mandy washed some vegetables and chopped them up very small, mixing them in with the cereal.

"You can give him wild plants, too," said Mandy. "As long as you don't pick them from the side of a busy road."

"Why not?" said Jack.

"Because they would be dirty and covered with car exhaust fumes," said Mandy.

"What kind of wild plants?" Jack asked.

"Oh, dandelions and dock leaves and clover," said Mandy. "But not too much clover. And definitely not buttercups. They'd make him sick. I can show you some if you like."

Jack shook his head. "There's so much to learn," he said.

Mandy nodded. "I know," she said. "But you'll soon get used to looking after him."

Jack fitted the water bottle onto the wire mesh of the hutch and they stood back and looked at it.

"Have we forgotten anything?" he asked.

Mandy shook her head. "I don't think so,"

she said. She frowned. "He'll need a piece of wood or a branch to gnaw on so that his teeth don't get too long. But that can wait."

"So, can we put him in his new home now?" said Jack, bursting with impatience.

Mandy smiled at him. "*You* can," she said. "He's your pet."

Jack bent down and carefully took Hoppy out of the carrier. He stood for a moment stroking his ears before he opened the door of the hutch and placed the little creature gently inside.

"My pet," he said. "And I'm going to take such good care of him."

9

The Race

Mandy hardly saw James for the next week. Every spare moment he could get he spent practicing for the go-cart race. One day he came to Animal Ark — to see if she would help him.

"Do you want me to time you?" Mandy said.

James nodded. "Down Beacon Hill," he said. "I borrowed a stopwatch from Dad."

So Mandy spent the next few days timing James as he raced down Beacon Hill in *Chee-tah*. He wasn't the only one. Andrew was there, and Peter and a few other boys, including Gary Roberts. Pam and Jill had decided to enter as well. Pam's mom was doing a night class in carpentry and had helped Pam with her go-cart. It was painted in tiger stripes and looked good. Gary's was painted to look like a snake. But Jill's looked a bit strange. It was painted to look like a car.

"It was my cousin's," she explained. "I just got it yesterday. I haven't had time to paint it yet."

"You don't have to," said Gary. "Just pretend it's a jaguar."

"Oh, great idea," laughed Jill. "Like a Jaguar car. I think your snake looks really good, Gary."

"It's an anaconda," Gary said proudly.

The air was filled with shouts as they all raced one another again and again.

"Just watch out for the river," Mandy yelled as James raced past her for a third time. "I don't want to have to fish you out."

By the time the day of the picnic came they were all in good shape. But Mandy thought James and Andrew were the best drivers.

"Of course you've practiced enough," Mandy said to James as they stood at the starting line on Beacon Hill. "Grandpa says you're a great driver."

James looked down at *Cheetah*.

"It really is a terrific go-cart," he said.

There was a huge banner saying ANIMAL AN-TICS stretched across the starting line. It had pictures of animals crawling and jumping and running in and out of all the letters. The sun was shining and Welford Village School was having the best picnic ever.

Beacon Hill sloped all the way down to the bridge over the river. Andrew, Peter, and James had marked out the course for the go-cart race with colored flags on poles.

"It looks really professional," Mandy said to Sarah Drummond beside her.

Sarah nodded. "Just as long as nobody goes into the river," she said.

"Mrs. Gardiner made sure the course went in the other direction at the bottom," James said.

The girls looked. The course followed the slope of the hill down to the bottom, then turned off in a wide sweep well away from the river.

"Look!" said Sarah. "The go-carts are starting to line up."

"Better get going, James," said Amy Fenton, walking up to them.

"Wish me luck," James said to Mandy.

Mandy grinned. "Good luck!" she said.

Then Mrs. Garvie asked the racers to line up at the starting line beside their go-carts. Mandy watched as everyone stood beside their go-carts, ready to jump into them and take off as soon as Mrs. Garvie blew the whistle. The seconds stretched out. Then the whistle blew — and they were off!

Mandy stood at the starting line with Sarah
and Amy, eyes glued to the go-carts racing
down the hill.

Andrew, James, and Peter were out in front
but Pam's go-cart had gathered speed and was
catching up. Jill had some trouble as she and
Gary veered toward each other. For a moment
it looked as if they would collide. Then Jill
straightened up and shot down the hill after the
leaders. James was neck and neck with Andrew

now. It was hard to tell which of them was ahead.

"Come on, James! Come on!" Mandy yelled, jumping up and down.

All around her people were yelling their heads off as the go-carts raced down the grassy slope. First one, then another edged in front. Pam's *Tiger* picked up speed, threatening to overtake *Kingfisher*. Andrew's blue go-cart looked very impressive with its chrome wheels flashing in the sunlight. Then *Cheetah* came up from behind *Kingfisher*.

"Look, James has just slipped into the lead!" said Sarah.

Mandy shaded her eyes from the sun to see better.

"Come *on*, James," she yelled again.

Cheetah sped on, its wheels sparkling in the sun, covering the ground faster than before. James was going to win! He was leaving Andrew behind!

Then Peter's *Terrier* put on a sudden burst of

speed and flashed past both *Cheetah* and *King-fisher*.

"*Terrier* in the lead," Amy shouted. "Go for it, Peter!"

But then disaster struck. Peter's go-cart went over a bump and spun around right in front of *Cheetah*. James swerved, just missing him. But he had lost ground and they were almost at the finish line. *Kingfisher* swooped past and crossed the line in first place.

The other go-carts were catching up as they swept down the hill behind James, but he managed to stay in front. James came in second, right on Andrew's heels.

The watchers cheered from the hilltop.

"Bad luck, James," Mandy said.

"If *Terrier* hadn't crashed, *Cheetah* might have won," said Amy.

"Do you think Peter is okay?" asked Mandy.

Jill nodded as Peter picked himself up and waved to the crowd. "Looks like it," she said.

Mandy watched them all trudge back up the

hill pulling their go-carts. They seemed to have enjoyed the race.

"You did great, James," said Mandy as James came up. "I think you did really well to come in second."

"So do I," said James. "I can't wait to tell your grandpa!"

"I won! I won!" Laura Baker shouted, running over the grass toward Mandy.

Mandy looked down at the little girl.

"I won the hedgehog race," said Laura. "I can roll better than anybody else."

Mandy looked at the grass stains on Laura's shorts. "I can see that, Laura," she said, laughing.

Sarah Drummond pushed a trolley full of packed lunches and cartons of juice over to them.

"Mrs. Garvie says we can have one more race before the picnic," she said to Mandy. "What should it be?"

Mandy looked at the clipboard she was holding.

"The rabbit race," she said.

"The rabbit race!" Laura yelled. "Wow! I bet I'll win."

And she raced off to the starting line. Mandy watched her go. Laura was full of energy.

"I've brought Hoppy," said a voice beside her.

Mandy looked around. Jack was standing there with Hoppy's carrier box in his arms. He opened the lid for Mandy to see.

"Oh, he's lovely," said Mandy, tickling Hoppy under the chin. "And look how much he's grown!"

The little rabbit twitched his ears and rubbed his nose with his tiny paws.

"He can run really fast now," said Jack. "I'm sure he'll win."

Mandy was puzzled. "Win what, Jack?" she said.

"The rabbit race," Jack said.

Mandy blinked. "But it isn't a *real* rabbit race," she said. "It's like all the other races. You have to pretend you're an animal and race that way."

"You mean it isn't a race for rabbits?" Jack said.

Mandy shook her head. "It's for people, Jack," she said. "Look!"

Mandy and Jack watched as Mrs. Garvie blew the whistle for the race to start. It was a sack race. The line of competitors hopped across the start, holding on to their sacks. Some of them wore silly paper rabbit ears. "Oh," said Jack. "I wondered why I couldn't see any other rabbits."

Mandy bit her lip. He looked so disappointed.

"I'm sure if we did have a real rabbit race Hoppy would win," she said.

There was a yell from the finish line and Mandy saw Amy Fenton throw herself across the line just in front of Laura. When she looked back, Jack had gone.

"Picnic time!" Mrs. Garvie called. Soon there was a stampede toward Sarah and the table full of goodies.

Mrs. Black, James's teacher, and Mrs. Todd,

Mandy's teacher, started handing out sand-
wiches and cartons of juice.

By the time Mandy had gotten something to
eat and sorted out the running order of the rest
of the races, she had forgotten all about Jack.

She was lining people up for the snake race
after lunch when the little boy appeared beside
her.

"Can I be in the race?" he said.

"Sure," said Mandy. She looked at Hoppy.
"Just make sure Hoppy is safe in his carrier box
first."

Jack ran off and Mandy turned back to
the children again. "You've got to wriggle,"
she told them. "No running and no crawling."

Everyone looked up at her seriously.

"How about rolling?" Laura said.

"No rolling," Mandy said firmly.

Mrs. Garvie put her whistle to her lips.

"Ready?" she said to Mandy.

Jack arrived at a run and slid down among
the other competitors on the grass.

"Ready!" said Mandy and Mrs. Garvie blew her whistle.

Everyone started wriggling.

"Look at that!" said Gary Roberts. "Maybe I should have brought Gertie along after all to show them how it's done."

Mandy, James, Sarah, and Andrew stood on the starting line, laughing. Children were all over the place, squirming and wriggling their way along the ground.

"Look at little Susan Davis," said James. "She's gone right off the course."

Mandy looked how Susan had wriggled her way right to the edge of the hill where the go-carts were parked.

"Stop! Susan!" shouted Andrew. "Watch out for the carts!"

Susan turned at the sound of his voice and rolled backward into Andrew's go-cart. It rocked slightly and she put out her hand.

They all watched as the go-cart slowly started to move downhill.

"Oh, no," said Andrew. "I must have left the brake off!" He ran off after his go-cart.

There was a clamor of voices as people turned to look at *Kingfisher* rolling down the hill, starting to go faster.

Then a terrified voice shouted over the others. "Hoppy!" Jack yelled.

Mandy spun around as the little boy jumped to his feet and began to run after the go-cart.

"Jack! What is it?" she yelled, running after him.

Jack didn't stop. "I put Hoppy in that go-cart," he panted as he ran. "I thought he would be safe."

Mandy looked at the go-cart racing down the hill — heading straight for the river. "James!" she screamed. "We must catch that cart."

James was already racing toward her, but she couldn't stop. If anything happened to *this* pet,

Jack would never be brave enough to get another.

Jack was fighting back tears. "He'll be killed, won't he?" he said as he stumbled across the grass. "If the go-cart goes into the river Hoppy will drown!"

10

Runaway Rabbit!

James ran to his go-cart and dragged it to the edge of the slope.

"What are you doing?" yelled Mandy.

"I'm going to try and cut off Andrew's go-cart before it gets to the river," he shouted back.

"I'll get my bike," she called. But James was already heading downhill in his cart.

Mandy saw James race off. His go-cart sped over the grass like a real cheetah. Andrew was halfway down the hill, making for his go-cart. Mandy made a dash for her bike and set off down the path that wound its way around the hill.

Down and down she went, hair flying, legs pumping the pedals. Behind her others raced, all trying to catch up with the runaway go-cart. Mandy lost sight of James as the path took her behind the hill. Then she was back on the same side again.

James had passed Andrew and was gaining on the go-cart. But would he be in time? *King-fisher* was getting nearer and nearer the river.

Once again the curve of the hill hid Mandy's view. The next time she came around James was swerving toward the runaway go-cart, cutting across its path in a desperate attempt to stop it. Mandy held her breath as she saw James's go-cart cut in front of Andrew's. There was a crash as the carts collided. Then James tumbled out of his seat and lay, perfectly still, on the grass. *Kingfisher* and *Cheetah* rolled on toward the river and came to a stop almost at the edge of the riverbank.

Mandy covered the rest of the distance between her and James at record speed.

"James!" she yelled. "Are you all right?"

James raised his head. "Don't stop! Get Hoppy!" he said.

Mandy raced on toward the overturned *Kingfisher*. Behind her, the others rushed up, shouting questions, bending over James.

Mandy leaped off her bike as she reached the entangled go-carts.

"Is my go-cart okay?" said Andrew, racing up.

"Your go-cart can be fixed," Mandy said, searching through the jumbled carts.

"What about Hoppy?"

She looked around as a small figure came running down the hill.

"Hoppy!" cried Jack. "Where's Hoppy?"

Mandy looked at *Kingfisher*. Had Hoppy fallen out? Had the go-carts crushed him?

Then she saw the edge of the carrier box, half wedged under a wheel. Holding her breath, she lifted the box up and opened the flap. There, shivering inside the box, was Hoppy. He was terribly frightened — but he was alive!

James arrived, limping slightly, as Jack peered into the carrier box, his eyes huge with fear.

"He's all right," Mandy said gently. "Just a little scared."

"Hoppy!" cried Jack. He gathered the rabbit up carefully in his arms and looked at James.

"You saved him," he said. "He was heading for the river. You stopped Andrew's go-cart. You saved his life, James. Thank you!"

James blushed bright red. "Don't mention it," he said.

But Mrs. Garvie had seen everything. She came bustling up to them.

"Are you hurt, James?" she said quickly. "You were limping."

James shook his head. "I just twisted my ankle," he said. "It's nothing."

"Nonsense," she said. "You're a hero, James."

James blushed even more.

"I bet that's the first time a cheetah beat a kingfisher to catch a rabbit," Peter Foster said and everybody laughed.

Mrs. Garvie looked serious for a moment. "I don't want anything like that ever to happen again," she said. Then she smiled.

"But since it *has* happened I think we'll

award a special prize for the most exciting race of the day."

Mandy looked at Jack. He was cuddling Hoppy close to his chest. The rest of the pupils gathered around. Jack's face glowed with happiness as he proudly showed off his pet.

Laura stood by his side. But Laura wasn't his only friend now. Jack was one of them now — one of the crowd. And so was Hoppy.

"A special prize would be great," Mandy said, looking at James. "A prize for the runaway rabbit race!"

coming soon

by Ben M. Baglio

The Hope family had just finished dinner when the phone rang.

"I'll answer it." Mandy ran through the hall.

"Mandy!" It was Grandma and she sounded worried.

"What's up?" Mandy asked.

"It's Frisky," Grandma said. "There's something wrong with him. Can you get Mom or Dad to come and take a look at him?"

"Oh, yes, of course," Mandy said. "We'll come right away." Her stomach turned over. She didn't think she could bear it if Frisky was sick.

She dashed back into the kitchen.

"Mom, Dad," she gasped. "Can you come with me to Grandma's? There's something wrong with Frisky."

"Oh, dear." Dr. Emily took off her apron. "I'll go. Dad can stay here in case there are any emergency calls. Is that all right, Adam?"

Dr. Adam was sitting at the table reading his vet's magazine. "Yes, go ahead. I hope Frisky's all right."

"Oh, so do I," Mandy said.

"We'll take the car," Dr. Emily said when they got outside. "Just in case Frisky needs to come back to the clinic."

Mandy felt very worried as she climbed into the car next to her mom. Frisky had been all right when she and James were at Lilac Cottage earlier.

They found Grandma waiting for them when they arrived. She hurried up the stairs in front of them and thrust open the door to Frisky's room.

"I think he's got mumps," she said anxiously.

Dr. Emily took one look at Frisky and burst out laughing.

"It's not funny, Emily!" Grandma sounded indignant. "Look at him!"

Frisky was sitting on top of his nest-box. He gazed at them with beady, bright eyes. His face was huge. His cheeks were puffed out to three times their normal size.

"Oh, Mom!" Dr. Emily laughed and shook her head. "He hasn't got mumps; he's storing food in his cheek pouches!"

"What?" Grandma was peering at Frisky with a worried look on her face.

Dr. Emily quickly told Grandma that hamsters have large pouches in their cheeks in

which to keep food. She pointed to his store
in the corner. "They have a food store, too.
Look."

Grandma began to laugh, too. "Oh, dear,"
she said, wiping her eyes. "What a silly woman
I am." She turned to Mandy. "Honestly, Mandy,
I know absolutely nothing about hamsters."

"Never mind, Grandma," Mandy said.

"Look," Grandma said, "I've got an idea.
Why don't you come and stay here for your vacation, Mandy? You could be full-time resi-
dent hamster-keeper for me." She turned to
Mandy's mom. "What do you think, Emily?"

"I think it would be a nice idea," Dr. Emily said. "It's not much fun at Animal Ark at the moment with ladders and cans of paint all over the place. How about it, Mandy?"

Mandy's eyes were shining. Stay with Grandma and look after Frisky for a whole week? It would be fantastic. "Oh, Mom," she said. "Can I really?"

Dr. Emily gave her a hug. "Really," she said. "It will save you from running over here every five minutes."

"Hear that, Frisky?" said Mandy. "I'm going to stay here and look after you."

Frisky gazed at her and twitched his nose.

Mandy looked up at her grandma. "He says it's a good idea."

Grandma chuckled. "I can see he's going to have the vacation of a lifetime."

"Yes," Mandy said. "And so am I."